Praise for Adam Cesare &
THE FIRST ONE YOU EXPECT

"In *The First One You Expect*, Adam Cesare displays an equal love and knowledge of the horror and noir genres, but what really sets this slim novel apart from other books of its type is Cesare's unflinching gaze at the life of a person willing to sacrifice everything for a dream. It's as emotionally devastating as the work of James M. Cain, but with all the violence and sleaze of *Tales from the Crypt*. I read *The First One You Expect* in a single sitting, and loved every moment of it."

—Cameron Pierce, editor of *In Heaven, Everything Is Fine: Fiction Inspired by David Lynch*

"Cesare's the young guy with the greatest encyclopedic gorehound know-how, blistering cinematic pace, unquenchable love of both fiction and film, and hell-bent will to entertain."

—John Skipp, *New York Times* bestselling author

"An engaging, contemporary thriller with a cutting-edge narrative, and characters so real they could live next door."

—Rio Youers, author of *Westlake Soul*

A Broken River Books original

Broken River Books
103 Beal Street
Norman, OK 73069

Cover art and design copyright © 2014 by Matthew Revert
www.matthewrevert.com

Interior design by J David Osborne

ISBN: 978-0-9994519-5-3

Printed in the USA.

# THE FIRST ONE YOU EXPECT

## ADAM CESARE

BROKEN RIVER BOOKS
NORMAN, OK

To any horror fan that picks up this crime book and then recognizes a part of themselves in the characters.

I hope it's not one of the awful parts.

# ONE

Sometimes late at night, I'll try to think of the exact points that I could change about my life to stop me from getting where I am.

Not some *Doctor Who* shit like going back in time to change the future. Just a message I could send to my younger self, just some tiny alteration I could have made in high school, maybe even earlier, that would have gotten me where I want to be.

Or, at this point, just somewhere else.

I never dwell on the recent fuckups. I never lay in bed regretting a purchase made on Amazon. I never tell myself that I shouldn't have pushed her. I go way back, say that I wouldn't have pushed her *if* I had asked the right girl to the prom. I wouldn't have pushed her *if* I had gone to college out of state. I wouldn't have pushed her *if* just one fucking person would have passed my script along to their bosses.

But, like I said, time travel is science fiction shit. I don't do science fiction. That stuff's for fat fags who jerk it to anime girls.

I'm a horror guy, I make horror movies and that's one thing I'd never change.

## TWO

Her tits are like flat tires. She's a stripper, but third-string and two years out of work. When I first sent her the email (a response to *her* response to my craigslist post) she sent me back a picture of herself with half a half-liter bottle of Coke. I'm not saying that it was half-full, just that half of it was obscured, in the picture.

She was my girl.

Well, one of them, not the first kill and certainly not the Final Girl, but one that could go somewhere in the middle. She wasn't going on the DVD box, that was for sure.

It took three messages back and forth to convince her that she would not have to suck any dick onscreen. It wasn't that she was averse to the idea, just that she was trying to gouge me on her daily rate.

There's no hardcore sex in my stuff, just simulated. Like the violence. I read somewhere that filmmaking is artful lying, and I always liked that. As sick as my shit gets, that quote is my true north. As long as it's all a lie, I'm still an artist and not some loser porn director.

"No. You sit down, and he comes from behind. You don't know he's there. Stop fucking looking," I yell, cutting the camera. We're shooting MiniDV, so there's no real reason for me to cut, but it saves me from watching this

3

useless footage later. I can't stand to hear my own voice on tape. I sound so whiny when I'm directing.

"Well I'm sorry, but I can hear him." She says, moving her hands up and down, her tits not bouncing but swinging like a perpetual motion machine. The way she talks with her hands makes me think that she's been living in the area her whole life, like me. Only she's had more time here than I have, she's over forty, has at least ten years on me. "If I can hear him shuffling around back there, isn't the audience going to hear him?"

"No. We'll fix it in post. Do what I tell you."

"We" will be me and I probably won't "fix it in post" beyond laying some music over it and hoping that the sound of Burt wriggling behind the couch isn't too bad. The music will be some local garage band grindcore or black metal shit. I don't much like any of that music, give me The Smiths or even The Misfits. I can't argue with it though, these bands not only let their music go for free, they also help promote the movie when it's released.

Like they think having a thirty second sample of one of their tracks in my movie is going to push them to superstardom.

Enjoy their music or not, those bands and I are in this together. We're all a part of the horror community. They sing about nun disfigurement, forced abortion and get some schmuck on Deviantart to do their album covers and they're automatically in the club. Makes me sick.

"One more time, then you're wrapped for today, sweetheart." I call all the girls sweetheart, it seems like the big time Hollywood thing to do, but using the nickname on this one turns my stomach.

"Burt, you good?" I ask.

"Yeah," I hear from behind the furniture. This couch has been in three of my features and two of my shorts. We need to find a new place to shoot. Either that or Burt needs a new couch.

I put my eye up to the viewfinder to check that everything's all good, and it is. The camera's set up on a tripod so I pop the screen out of it and watch on that instead of having to keep my eye jammed up against it and risk suffering a camera bump if I move my head.

"Action," I say. The stripper starts eating popcorn, her fingers are already greasy from the previous two takes, but nobody's going to notice that. They'll be too busy leering.

In the scene she's watching a scary movie by herself. Topless. As you do, or at least as they do in Tony Anastos films.

Tony's my stage name but Anastos is my real name. I figured I'd cut the Greek with a little Italian, even though I'm about as Italian as a gyro filled with souvlaki.

Burt creeps his hand over the back of the couch, feeling around like his fingers have got a mind of their own. He's such a ham, even when he spends most of the movie with a sock over his head. Cracks me up, that guy.

The lady is *ooo*-ing and *ahh*-ing at the screen, her face illuminated. Later tonight I'll shoot some inserts from her perspective, making sure that whatever's on the TV is out of copyright and in the public domain. *Night of the Living Dead*, maybe.

Right now there's daytime TV on. Ellen explains the douching process to the toad from *Dance Moms*. Or some shit like that, I can't tell because it's on mute. The stripper-broad does a good job reacting to the television it like it's the scariest shit she's ever seen.

Burt's gloved hand catches her by the shoulder and she turns. His fingers slip down a little bit, like they always seem to "in the heat of the moment." I tell him that he's going to get his ass kicked one day by one of these girl's boyfriends or maybe even the girls themselves. I tell him this, but I don't much care. In fact, him getting handsy adds realism.

What evil slasher maniac isn't going to take a quick squeeze?

I would.

He vaults over the back of the couch like he's a fucking Olympian, but he's not. The front feet of the couch rise up and smack down and the whole thing shakes, but the actors are both still in frame so it's all good.

She slaps at him and I can barely keep from laughing because she's really giving it to him. The back of her knuckles clip his jaw as she's winding up for another smack and the sound is priceless. I hope the microphone picks it up.

He throttles her, taking the knife out of its sheath and holding it up to one of her sagging breasts.

"I'm gonna make you eat your tits," he says. It's an adlib but a good one. We'll keep it, but we're not really going to make her eat her tits. Too expensive.

The thing about Burt's character, The Debaser, that I think is so great, is that he's part-slasher and part-serial killer. We don't have the budget for the big kills like Jason or Freddy, so our slasher's got a Manson/*Henry: Portrait of a Serial Killer* vibe to him. He talks to his victims, has a process. His kills are all true-to-life. And cheap.

People on the forums seem to like that. But then again, these are the same guys who pass each other bittorrent links to wartime snuff films and think that animated gifs of the 9/11 attacks set to the *Happy Days* theme are a riot.

I don't know if I'd ever want to hang out with them, but these sick fucks are my audience. Even if they're misunderstanding what I'm trying to do here, the message under all this corn syrup and simulated semen.

Burt grips her by the shoulder farthest from the camera and cheats her body towards me as he drags the knife along her neck.

What a pro.

The two fingers he'd got curled under the blade pump the Caro syrup down her throat and onto her tits. We hold for a minute and I unhook the base-plate, going handheld for a few shots of her corpse while the blood is still in roughly the same position.

I try to move quickly because I've cut the blood with a little water to thin it, make it pump better. If you leave the watered-down stuff on camera too long it starts getting too opaque.

Working my way up from the pool that's formed in her navel, I glide up and hold on her face. It's like a staring contest, me with my eye pressed up to the viewfinder and her trying her damndest not to blink. When she finally does I cut the camera and stand up.

Burt's already got a towel for her. She says thanks and I don't ruin the moment by telling her that Burt's more concerned with not staining his couch than he is with her comfort. We've got to do something about this fucking couch.

"That's a wrap for you, Doll."

I don't tell her about the extra scene we're going to shoot with the fake head. The latex face doesn't much resemble her but I'm going to put a wig on it to get the hair color right, at least. Then Burt's going to pluck her eyeball out, a sheep's eye that I've ordered from a company that sells lab supplies to schools, and then he's going to mess around with the socket. The extra gore not only gives the sickos something to savor, but pads the runtime.

Once we hit seventy something minutes this puppy is feature length and we can get to work on the next one.

I give her the two hundred we agree on and write her name down to be sure it's spelled the way she wants it in the credits. When Burt leaves the room to go get some wet paper-towels for the upholstery, she offers to blow me for an extra fifty.

She makes me sad, but that pang of self-loathing doesn't stop me from taking her up on the offer.

## THREE

I've got a significant following online, but money's still tight so I work as a cashier down at Stop & Shop. It was a job that was brutally depressing after high school but isn't that bad now that most of the people I know have either moved away or become equally depressing themselves.

It makes for good people-watching, and some of my coworkers aren't total wastes of life. Burt's not bad, of course. He's a fun guy, used to be even more fun when he was sober part of the time. He's a friend and a fan. I pay him a quarter of what the girls get, which usually amounts to half a pizza and a six pack after a day of shooting.

I don't drive, so it also helps that Burt has a car.

My manager is a nice older lady named Deloris. She owns (and claims to love) all of my films. It's strange for a sixty-something woman to enjoy watching strippers dismembered for seventy five minutes, but it takes all kinds I suppose.

One time she let me use the deli counter and backroom for a shoot, which is more than my own mother's ever done for my work. The cold cuts that come out of the slicer still taste a bit like latex. Deloris is all right.

What I do at the store mainly consists of three things: scanning UPCs, punching in the codes for produce and asking customers if they've got a Super Saver card. Even

9

if they don't have the membership card, I run one for them anyway. This is Deloris's policy and she claims that it promotes customer loyalty.

Occasionally I'll be told to train a new cashier, something that I'm asked to do this morning while I'm clipping my nametag onto my green Stop & Shop polo. The nametag says Tony, even though my paystubs are made out to Nicholas Anastos.

Over the last few years, I've begun to think as Tony Anastos with Nicky fading from my consciousness. Nicholas now seems like a kid I used to know in grade school that moved away. I sign my emails as Tony, take calls as Tony and one day I plan on changing it over legally. It's like Tony is Nicholas's cooler older brother.

"Tony, this is Anna, please show her the ropes." Deloris says.

I turn and see Anna. She's young but not high school-young, which is a relief, because she's gorgeous.

"Tony's been part of the family here for years, but now he's only part-time because he directs independent films."

Deloris is lying, as if even she is ready to admit how pathetic working at this place for fifteen years is. My hours are reduced, but I'm still full-time. It's the only way to get benefits. She knows that, but she's just helping me out with this girl.

"Nice to meet you," I say, the words coming out *meetchew*. It's to the point where I can no longer tell whether I'm trying to put on the Long Island accent or not. I tell myself that I don't really have one, could stop if I wanted to, but I no longer have to think about using it and that scares me.

She says the same thing. Then I ask, "Have you worked a register before?"

"Back in high school, at Rita's over the summer."

That's nice, she's pointing out how old she is, wants me to take note that she's street-legal. A good sign. Her hair is long and black with bleach blonde highlights, so many highlights that it's hard to tell whether she's a blonde with black roots or a brunette with blonde tips. There's a ring of cursive inked on her left wrist, the writing so tiny that I can't make it out. Either that or it's Elvish. There are more tattoos under that polo, I know it.

She'd look good on a DVD case, has a real alt-girl vibe. That's hot with the nerds. A real life Suicide Girl next door.

"The custard's good there, at Rita's," I say, even though I've only had it a handful of times and it never satisfies me like real ice cream does.

When Anna isn't watching, Deloris shoots me a look that tells me she thinks that Anna and I would have cute kids. Deloris is constantly wheedling me about whether I'm seeing anyone. One time she told me a story about her gay nephew and how much she loves him. I think she made the guy up just to check if I was a homo, because she never mentioned him again.

Girls are expensive and time-consuming, so I don't date much. That's what I tell myself, not Deloris. I'd rather put the money towards my next production, or something else, something tangible.

I explain the sign-in system to Anna and she stands behind me as I take a few customers. It's all pretty self-explanatory. It has to be since many of the cashiers are high school kids, most of them stoned out of their minds.

When there's a lull I say: "If anyone asks you for something and you don't know where it is, just send them to an aisle that's far enough away from your register that they probably won't come back and ask you again."

She laughs at this, but I'm not kidding.

"What kind of movies do you make?" she asks.

Oh, that moment.

I'm not asked often, as I don't find myself in many situations with unfamiliar people. What I usually say is "scary stuff," but Anna looks like she can get down, so I'm honest with her.

"I make microbudget horror films." I say. There's a twinkle in her eyes that I can't tell from the real thing. I'm no good at reading girls.

"Yeah. Me and my friend Burt have a series of movies starring a character called The Debaser. He works here, too. The tall, goofy guy stocking produce." I point towards Burt but he's not there, may as well be imaginary.

"Just you two?" she asks. "That must be a lot of work."

"That or the movies aren't very good," I say and she touches my shoulder, like she doesn't want the self-deprecating act. It's a bummer, because that's my only act. "Our movies are really small. We find most of our actors on Craigslist, we don't pay much."

"I'd like to see them sometime."

I offer to bring her a copy of my best one and she smiles.

# FOUR

There are numbers on their spines.

If they weren't numbered, didn't line up so nicely on a shelf, I wouldn't have a hundred fifty dollars worth of Blu-ray discs in my online shopping cart.

It would be a real shame to have them all on the shelf except a few numbers. That would be nuts.

It's possible, that in a world where they didn't have numbers on their spines, I may not even be this drunk right now. It's tough to tell, it may be a chicken/egg situation. Do I drink because it better enables me to buy shit I can't afford or is the buying a result of my alcohol dependency?

Whatever.

I hit the one-click checkout button after setting the default card to one that won't be declined, then close out the browser tab before I can read the final total. They have to charge tax now when shipping to New York. The fuckers.

That box will show up in two days and I won't remember having ordered it, but I'll be glad that I did. For a day, at least. I'm not worried about it arriving and having my parents see it. I rent from them, live in the basement, but they both work more hours than me so odds are that I'll have the box inside and open before my mother has a chance to hassle me about it.

I've got maybe two fingers of Steel Reserve left in the can, so I finish it and click over to Twitter. I send out a bunch of messages to *Dread Central* and *Bloody Disgusting*, calling them out for not running news about my movies. They could at least review the discs I send them.

*Why no support for independent art @Mattfini? Fucking sellout. Too much of a pussy for THE DEBASER?*

It's all boilerplate stuff, and I don't really mean it, but it feels good to let the venom out. I have over five hundred followers, but I'm following nearly two thousand people. It's not the ratio I want.

After that's done for the night, the room's spinning.

Half-hard, I try looking for Anna on facebook but realize that I don't remember her last name. That or I didn't know it to begin with. So instead I pull up Final Cut, trimming the footage we shot the other day while I jerk off.

## FIVE

"You can't be serious," Burt says.

He isn't as big a fan of the idea as I am.

"Look, she's right. We need to get with the times," I say. "A female slasher? A sexy female slasher? You know how those internet assholes eat up that 'Women in Horror' shit. There's a whole month dedicated to it, shit's bigger than prostate cancer month. The idea's a goldmine. We're being progressive!"

"Kickstarter though? Are we that desperate?" Burt says, trying to hide the fact that what he's really upset about is losing his place as our star.

He doesn't give a shit about us trying to use Kickstarter to get some extra money, he had suggested the same thing himself a few weeks ago. I even got far enough along with the idea that I created an account and applied.

"The Debaser is going to be in it." I say. "It's not like you're out of a job."

"I read the script, Tone. You fucking kill him." Reading isn't Burt's strong suit, so I'm amazed that he's cracked open the file I sent him already. It wasn't a script, though, just a rough outline.

Burt's a few years older than me, we met in high school and he was a super senior when I was a sophomore. We didn't start really hanging out until after school, but I knew him enough to know that he was in mixed classes, needed things slowed down for him so he could understand them. Dyslexia, maybe? He's not dumb, just unlucky.

"It's a passing of the torch. And yeah, which slasher hasn't died a few times? Cool your tits."

Turns out Anna liked the movie I gave her. A lot. Enough that she wants to help out.

And I wasn't too far off with that Suicide Girl observation. She says that soon she's moving to the city to be a model. I knew a few girls like that in school. They're not models now.

So it's just me connecting dots that she has already hinted at connecting when I say that she should be an actress. She says something like how she doesn't think she has the talent, but I reassure her.

Then the rest of it is all her idea, something she clearly had planned before I brought up her trying her hand at acting, and I listen to what she has to say, the two of us alone in the staffroom, her drinking water from a paper cone.

I know I'm being played. I know that. But the idea is so good.

And her lips are full and moist from the water.

## SIX

The discs aren't my only collection. No, I have many more things that I blow my no-money on.

I've got more posters than can fit on my walls, the most valuable of which are in tubes in my closet because I haven't gotten around to getting them framed. There are two milk crates under my bed filled with magazines, some of them rare German splatter zines, the kind of stuff that my mom leafed through once when I wasn't at home and ended up calling the cops on me.

I wasn't arrested, it's not like I had a Michael Jackson treasure trove under there, but the cops did talk to me for a good long time. We stood there in the basement, them pawing through my stuff, creasing the corners of every fucking thing they touched.

That's where my knife collection comes in.

It's the only non-horror thing I collect, but I like to think that the blades are at least tangentially related to my other hobby.

They're all real, unlike the props that we use in The Debaser movies. Artful lying, as I said, there's no room on set for real knives if they're going to pose a risk to any of my actors. Safety to people. That's Lloyd Kaufman's first

17

rule of indie filmmaking. In many ways Lloyd's full of shit, but that's one area where it's worth listening to him.

The knife collection is what kept the cops there, grilling me. If it were just the magazines, they probably would have laughed at my batshit mother and apologized to me for the inconvenience. She thinks I'm some kind of serial-killer-in-training because of the stuff I collect. When the cop flipped open the leather suitcase I stash in the TV cabinet, that's when their questions got serious.

*Where did you get all these blades?*

I go to convention in Jersey every year, there's a guy there that sells knives. He sells bootleg DVDs too, but I don't tell the cops that.

It was tough to explain that I just like them. That, okay, one time I did use them in one of my movies, but just as set dressing, a single shot of The Debaser looking at his knife collection and selecting the best one for the job. The knife he chose was one of our screen-ready knives, of course, one with a dummy blade so dull that you couldn't even prepare a salad with it.

Now I'm standing in the room and watching Anna go through the stuff.

It's the first time in years that anyone beyond Burt and my mother has been down here. I don't invite my mother in, of course, but I know she's down here when I'm not home. Checking for bodies, tossing out empties, and weeping for little Nicholas, who had been such a bright boy.

My father's not on my side, but he doesn't think I'm the next Dahmer, either. To him, I just exist, the same way that Vinny Testaverde exists. But Vinny doesn't play for The Jets anymore and I never did, so neither of us much rates.

Anna is touching everything, but unlike the cops she's gentle, she's got a collector's hands. Burt's gentle too, but even he'll crease a corner every now and again, place a disc the wrong way in a jewelcase.

I can't tell if the basement smells like dried load or whether it's my imagination. It's clean enough. I emptied the garbage pail this morning, spritzed some Frebreze onto my sheets and the canvas of my desk chair.

"Holy shit," she says, clicking open the briefcase. It could be the kind of *holy shit* that means she's beginning to think of me like my mother does, or it could be something else.

She lifts up a blade and pops open both sides of it. The one she's holding, it's made to look like a batarang. Not the Adam West kind, but the Christian Bale kind. Both ends are sharp as hell, the wings extending into four inch blades on each end, so you can grip it around the bat and have a weapon on either side of your fist.

"This is really cool," she says, the enthusiasm in her voice almost bordering on valley girl for a moment. How many parts are there to this girl? "What do you, ya know, use it for?"

"I don't. They're collectibles."

"Sending your kids through college with these?" She says, whirling her fist around, pointing at everything in the room with the tips of the blades. Something about her scares me and turns me on at the same time. I want to backhand her and kiss her deep. But I won't, of course.

I'm no good with women.

"So where's your camera?" she asks, folding up the batarang and removing my Bowie knife from its sheath. I call that one Rambo. They don't all have names, that would be silly, but that one does.

"Why?"

"Because we should shoot some footage before we make the actual Kickstarter video, right? A screen test to see how the costume looks. I read something like that online." She pats the backpack she brought with her. She's been dropping lines like this all day, how she's been doing research online. Where exactly does one go to find out about this stuff in such a short amount of time?

"You have a costume?" This is news to me, but somehow it shouldn't be. Anna is big into her character already and we haven't even come up with a name yet. In the pages I was working on I just call her ANNA, planning on pulling a find/replace when we decide on a name.

I open my closet and reach to the top shelf. I have to climb on two milk crates to reach, it's embarrassing. I can feel her eyes on me as I go to my tippy-toes, my shirt lifting up and my belt sagging so that I can feel my exposed lower back. I know that from where she's standing she can see my hairy crack. I start to sweat.

Using the shoulder strap, I bring the camera bag down and try to dismount with some modicum of grace. I turn around and she already has clothes from her backpack lying out on my bed. It doesn't seem like she's been watching me climb into the closet, which is good.

"Turn it on," she says. I unzip the camera bag, slide the battery into place and open the viewfinder.

There's the familiar ding and I nod to her. "It's going. Action."

"Hello world, I'm Anna Diamond and this is Cat Killer's first screen test."

Where are these names coming from? Her last name's not really Diamond, it's Friedman, I asked Deloris. Cat Killer? Is that my new character? The only thing that pisses me off about it is that I wasn't allowed to think of it. Other than that, it's great.

She peels off her shirt and I feel blood rush everywhere. I'm a pale guy and I blush easy. I imagine that my face looks like I'm choking.

She's wearing a black bra, but it's see-through. Her areolas are large and light. She's got a tattoo running up her side from her bottom rib and headed down her jeans. I feel like I'm going to pass out.

I'm never alone with them, Burt's always there. I'm never not paying them, either.

Taking a tanktop from the bed, she slips it on. It's got holes in it, the print faded. It could be something from her own wardrobe or something that she's weathered for this photo shoot.

The jeans go next, she's so quick to wiggle out of them that her panties slip down and I see the top of her pubic hair. It's trim, orderly, but still dark. It's like she's been reading my diary.

Troma-green fishnets under a simple black skirt. It works.

"And?" she says. Her fingers and arms are spread, she stands pushing her breasts out. The camera soaks her in,

I can practically hear the gulping sounds it's making. Or maybe that's me.

"Well, the tanktop's the problem. We can't use the Nirvana smiley face without paying for it. If you got a plain one." Before I can finish, she's bent down, her ass to the camera, showing us how short the skirt is and digging through her backpack. The shirt's off again and replaced with a plain black tank top before I have time to get embarrassed by her nudity.

"Better?" she asks.

I use the slider on top of the camera to zoom to her face. She's smiling and I go wider again. By the time I'm zoomed back to a medium shot, she's got Rambo tucked between her skirt and her bare skin. I jump.

"Be careful with that. It's sharp!"

She tells me that she knows, and then we spend the next hour running through adlibs, trying to find Cat Killer's style.

## SEVEN

As soon as she leaves I call up Burt and tell him to come over. Or come pick me up and drive me to his place. Whatever, we need to hang out.

It's his place.

He pours us both a drink and I show him all the footage. The look in his eyes tells me that he's a true believer and he sips deep from his Solo cup full of screwdriver.

"Dude, we work with that girl." He's either yelling at me or giving me a verbal thumbs-up, maybe both.

"But does she look like lunchmeat to you, or a star?"

"How much did you pay her?"

"For this? This is gratis. This is her career here, this is what she wants us to help her achieve."

"It's fishy, dude." Burt throws a "dude" in there when he thinks he's being serious. It just makes him sound like an asshole.

Burt drinks again, I drink too so that he doesn't feel self-conscious. I have a drinking and shopping problem, but Burt just has a drinking problem.

"We hashed out most of the script for the Kickstarter pitch," I say. "I say we ask for five grand, but I think we'll make more. A lot more."

"Panhandling."

23

"No. Utilizing the talent that's fallen into our lap. Hitching our star to her wagon." When I get serious, I talk in clichés.

"Your lap," Burt says and snaps out the back of his fingers for a sacktap, but I move and he gets my thigh. Still stings, though. It's a good thing that I'm friends with Burt, otherwise I would have stopped having my balls smacked in the 11th grade. This is his way, we're all stunted, the geeks and the weirdoes. I obsess about shit that doesn't matter, want to own more pressed plastic than everyone else, and Burt just wants a do-over on high school, maybe give his black sweatshirts and cigarettes a happy ending this time.

"I need more, you need more?" he asks and I shake my head.

I stay parked on Burt's couch as he gets up to pour some more vodka into a splash of orange juice. I look down at the upholstery and, yup, there are still speckles of pink from our last shoot. The spots depress me, make me think of my mother scrubbing our bathtub until she gets all of the pink out of the grout. I'm not allowed to shoot in the house any more, it's kind of the only term of my lease.

Thinking of my own mother makes me think of Burt's. He's got his own place alright, a level of autonomy that I don't have, but I wouldn't trade him. Because his mother died ten years ago. Lung cancer, she was skinny ever since I started hanging out with Burt and would catch glimpses of her, but in those last few months she'd shrink between my visits, until she was nothing, dead.

His dad had always been a space cadet, went even spacier after her dying like that, and moved into an apartment in Lindenhurst, leaving Burt the house. I don't think they're in contact, or at least I'm not kept up to speed on that stuff. We're friends, see each other a few hours a day, mimimum, but there's a bunch of aspects of Burt's life that I'm not privy to. Either that or they don't exist, he's just a lonely dude that doesn't exist when I'm not with him, just drinks and jerks off and channel surfs.

"Look, man," I start, trying to sound as sincere as possible. I like Burt. If I'm being honest, he's my only friend. "Why don't you slow down with that and we invite her over. She'd probably be down. We can watch a movie, talk a bit more about what we plan to do, involve you this time."

Asking Burt to slow down is one of his triggers, like I've offered him a fratboy dare. He upends his Solo cup, a stream of nearly-clear orange juice dribbling down his neck. "No, I don't think so," he says. Part of me is relieved, I don't want these two spending any more time together than absolutely necessary.

"This is a good thing for both of us and you need to see that."

Burt wipes himself with the bottom of his t-shirt.

"I do," he says after a moment. "I'm just jealous I didn't get to see Anna do her striptease act."

"You will," I reassure him, but part of me doesn't want him looking.

## EIGHT

That night I'm lying in bed and I see that I have a new follower on twitter. @Cat_Killer. Her profile picture is just cleavage, Rambo pressed over her chest.

I wonder when she took that picture, but not for long. I press the follow button and start reading over the tweets she's been sending out all day.

She's got ninety eight followers already, which doesn't even seem possible. It took me months to get that much momentum.

Under her info section she's described herself as "One Sick Psycho Killer Slut! *Star* of the New Movie from @ TonyAnastosfilmmaker!!!"

I click on my own name and, sure enough, I'm up about thirty followers.

It seems petty to think that my relationship with Anna has already borne me great fruit, thirty followers worth of fruit, but this is a new world. Social media's full of assholes with shitty opinions who can't spell worth a damn, but that doesn't mean I shouldn't be embracing it, getting myself out there.

I type up my own tweet.

"Be sure to follow @Cat_Killer, bitch is getting ready to cut you up. :)"

My stomach twitches as I type out the smiley face, cuteness gives me indigestion, but I read somewhere that people like that shit, it makes it more intimate, even from tough guys. Plus, the tweet is just as much for Anna as it is for my five-hundred mouth-breathers.

I plug my phone in, the cord running under my pillow, and pull the sheet up. I'm sober tonight and that makes it harder to sleep. I always take a night off the bottle when I see Burt drinking heavily. Earlier tonight he offered to drive me home, but I told him I'd walk, that I had a few phone calls to make and the night air would make me feel good. It's a long walk, one that takes me over Sunrise Highway on a skinny footbridge, but it's better than getting in a car with a wasted Burt.

Normally I'd have taken a swig of Nyquil, but I'm all out so now I'm lying in bed with my mind racing.

I usually love nights like this, nights when I'm full of ideas, because I won't sleep, but tonight it's different. If I'm excited about a project, I'll stay up until dawn working on the script, sometimes photoshopping a poster. I haven't been this wound up in a while.

I can't stay up tonight though, I shouldn't. I've got an early shift at Stop & Shop and then we're going to start working on the Kickstarter video.

My pillow buzzes and I check my messages. It's a text from Anna.

"Who u calling a bitch?"

Even though I just sent out the tweet, it takes me a second to register what she's referring to.

I start typing up a response, feeling a weight of dread pressing down on the happiness I was just skating across. Even after spending hours with her, going over character quirks and style tips and movies Anna should check out for inspiration, I still can't read her, know what's up with her.

"I was kidding, no offense. I was in character, you know? Since you call yourself a slut in ur profile."

It only takes a second for her response, but the lag feels immeasurable.

"A bitch and a slut are two different things." The grammar is perfect for a text, she even spelled out the number.

I can feel sweat slicking up my sheets, my neck oily. I should have showered.

"I'm sorry."

The response time is longer now, so long I lay there, unsure if one will come.

"I'm kidding, are you always such a pussy? Have a good night. :-P"

"Ha. Thanks, u 2. Big day tomorrow." I type back, ignoring the part about being called a pussy.

The sweat begins to cool but still leaves me sticky. I only sleep for about two hours.

# NINE

Burt has the stocking on the top of his head, pulled up around his eyebrows so that the end hanging off his hair looks like a spent condom. He's got his arms crossed in front of him, his forearms so long and skinny that crossing them he looks much less imposing than if he didn't. Glaring at me behind Anna's back, Burt's trying to stand still, but failing.

Burt showed up to set reeking of vodka.

Well, the set is his house, but he is drunk when Anna and I get there. After work I tell him that I don't need a ride to his place, that Anna's going to drive me. We show up forty minutes after him, stopping by my place to get the camera, and he's drunk when we arrive.

If my mother hadn't held us up on the way to Burt's, I could have been here in time to stop him from finishing the bottle.

My mother's eyes are a bit lighter as she talks to Anna. Without her Cat Killer costume on, Anna looks sweet, normal and Mom insists on calling me Nicky in front of her.

"What a lovely home you have, Mrs. Anastos." The words fit her so well that I can't believe this is the same girl who whirls around knives, is unashamed to let me see the

31

silky underwear she rocks, probably is still rocking now, as she butters up my mother.

As she points to the framed photos along the wall, marvels at the Grecian landscapes, I wonder which Anna is the closest to the real her, which one is the act.

"Am I in the fucking video or what?" Burt says.

"Not if you can't stand up straight," I say.

All three of us are quiet. We're down in Burt's basement, I shift and the grit from the packed-dirt floor crackles under my sneakers.

Anna looks at me, her expression a little worried, the first time I've seen her unsure of herself. I hate that Burt's done this to us.

"Look, just sober up. We'll film the sequences that don't need you, the straight up pitch stuff with Anna talking to the camera. We'll run through it a few times, catch a few different angles. If you go puke everything out, you should be ready to go in an hour, right?"

Burt is tapping his feet while I speak, right foot left foot. His eyes are all over the basement: to the boiler, to Anna's ass, to the boxes of junk labeled "mom" around us, but never meeting my stare. The guy's ashamed, the skin beneath his beard red and wet.

He doesn't say anything, just nods, swinging his hand over and catching the banister, the stairs rocking as he climbs back up into the house, leaving Anna and I alone in the basement.

There's a moment where neither of us speak, and the reality of the situation is apparent to me now. I have these depressing moments sometimes, not moments of doubt, exactly, more like moments of stark clarity. We're not on a film set. She's not an actor and I'm not a director. We're two people standing in a friend's basement. There's no glamour here, no one cares and I have the sick feeling that we're going to put this video up and get nothing. I'm usually alone when I realize these things, but now Anna's with me and that makes it so much worse.

I don't know whether to sob or smash the camera into her face and then hang myself with my belt. I wish I could tear my skin off.

I look at her, ready for her to say that she's realized it too, that there's nothing here that's going to further her career, that she's ready to leave. She can give up like I wish I could give up. She doesn't yet need a do-over on the last ten years.

"We don't need him anyway," she says and places a hand on my shoulder. Her heavy neo-Elvira makeup is warpaint that darkens her eyes. "We can do the video ourselves. You're going to make me a star, right?"

I nod.

"This place is great," she waves her arms at the basement and I see it, it *is* great. Production value out the ass, no extra lighting needed. I'm not a Tony Robbins guy, not a convert to the power of positive thinking, I just make my shit and try to sell it the best I can. But I do get low, sometimes. Blue. I'm glad she's here to bring me back, make me see the possibilities.

The house above us is quiet and I can hear the bathroom door close and Burt start the faucet running.

Hopefully he'll be able to clean himself out.


Anna has It and people will pay to watch more.

She inhabits the frame, even though we're only in one room, with only a few pieces of set dressing (a rubber severed hand from Party City's Halloween selection, a dull machete), Cat Killer is determined to get us our money.

"If we don't meet our goal in thirty days we won't receive any of the money. Scroll down to the sidebar and you'll see what kind of rewards we've got in store for you. DVDs, posters, signed eight-by-tens. And one very lucky donor could even get dinner with me. And don't even think of bringing me to some Vegan shithole. I want blood."

She smiles, we haven't scripted half of what we've got so far. It just rolls out of her. Her onscreen demeanor is a mix of Anna Diamond and Cat Killer, both girls a far cry from the sweet Anna Friedman who talked up my mother earlier today.

Maybe one day, after the movie is wrapped, I'll talk to her about the idea that we both share a weird form of split personality disorder. I can ask her who she thinks of herself as: Friedman or Diamond. Whether she's a Tony or a Nicholas. She'll understand it like she seems to get most things about me.

"This movie's going to have everything, it chronicles the demise of the musty has-been slashers and the rise of a new icon. But there is one aspect we're keeping old school: the gore. With your help, we're going to have mind blowing practical makeup effects. We need plaster, latex, paint and actors and that's the main reason why we need to raise five thousand dollars."

Behind the camera, I point up at the ceiling, indicating that we're shooting for more.

"This stuff is expensive, so we'd love it if we could reach more. In fact, for every thousand dollars we go over our initial goal, I'll be sending our backers a special picture, one less article of clothing for each thousand."

It's genius.

"But watching me stand around and look pretty is not all you want to see in this video, is it? You want to see me do my thing, right?"

She's looking directly into the camera, I can hear Burt flush the toilet upstairs, the mic picks it up but Anna seems unfazed. Burt has been up there for about ten minutes. At a certain point I thought I heard retching beneath the sound of the faucet, but it's hard to be sure. I hope that he's empty, ready for a cup of black coffee.

"Follow me," she says to the camera. Behind the viewfinder I hitch up an eyebrow. "Yes, you," she says, still playing with the audience but talking to me. She points to the stairs with the end of the machete and begins to climb up backward, feeling out each step with her heel, careful not to slip.

I follow her. I'm unsure where this is going.

"To prove how invested our writer-director Tony Anastos is in the quality of this film, he's left nothing to chance."

She's at the top of the steps now, the door is open and I can see the kitchen countertop from the viewfinder. It's breaking the illusion of the basement being some dark netherworld and also giving her some ugly backlighting. I'm not sure if I'm going to be using this footage in the video, but I let it roll to see where she's taking me.

"Most of you probably know The Debaser, you've followed his adventures for years and are probably no doubt looking forward to his return, maybe even as a special guest in my film."

She's through the kitchen doorway now, pulling the camera closer with one finger, turning her back so I can catch her skirt, the fabric bouncing against her ass, the fishnets tight against her legs.

I notice another aspect of her costume for the first time now, the sheath wrapped around her right thigh, half of it obscured by the skirt, giving her a pointed silhouette.

We're walking toward the bathroom. She stops in the first floor hallway, turns to address the camera.

"I've been reading your concerns on the message boards, how you're worried about the same old props, the same lame fake knives," she holds up the machete, then drags the dummy blade across her white wrist. The metal leaves a slight redness, but doesn't break the skin.

"Fucking nothing," she says, holding out the mild abrasion, then tossing the machete over her shoulder, putting a gash into the hallway molding that I can see from behind the camera.

"With your donation, we'll be able to afford premium props like this one." She flips up the side of her skirt and puts one hand on the sheath, removing Rambo with the other. When did she take it? Has she had it the entire time? Has she stolen from me?

I almost want to ask her, but my voice would ruin the take.

"A beauty, right? And *totally* unsafe around a crazy mother like me." She smiles and holds her arm out again, cutting the back of her arm with the blade. I take a quick hissing breath and her eyes dart up at me, warn me not to make any more noise. "Did I mention I'm a cutter?" Her voice is sweet and innocent, Muppet Babies Marilyn Monroe.

The wound is real, a two inch cut, not deep and too pale to show up on video at first. She uses the side of the blade to push down on her arm, the blood welling up in the cut, causing it to glow bright red.

The light in the hallway is shit, but she's positioned herself under the one bare bulb, given us the best lighting possible.

There's coughing from inside the bathroom, Burt is still in there. The faucet still running, a constant stream uninterrupted by the washing of hands. The sound makes me think that he's either still puking or passed out in front of the toilet.

"All you fanboys won't want The Debaser after what I'm about to show you."

She takes a step back, puts her free hand on the door, a thin line of blood traveling down her arm now, toward her elbow. She knocks and the blood drips, splashing onto the gold doorknob.

There's no answer from the bathroom and Anna pushes the door open. There's a split second where I'm really hoping I'm not about to see Burt on the toilet, taking a shit.

"And here he is. Our fearsome killer. Is this video canon?" she asks, not waiting for the reply. "Yup. This is the official, first ever unmasking of The Debaser. And, surprise! He's a drunk sack of shit."

I enter the room, Burt is laying next to the toilet, his eyes-half open. He's still got the stocking on his head.

He looks pathetic, my heart breaks for my friend, for his dead mom, and for what a shithead I've been to him for the last decade.

Would yelling "cut" stop his humiliation? Or would it just speed us on our way to the three-way argument that will no doubt come from Anna and I busting into the bathroom.

"What the fuck?" Burt says, the first word getting lost in a drool bubble. He has puked, I can smell it, but it hasn't made him very spritely. Not spritely enough to have flushed.

Anna ignores him, the smell, turns to the camera. She's yelling now, some James Dean method shit, her face red, a vein popping.

"You want a game-changing slasher like The Burning or The Prowler? Have you had it with that DIY made-in-a-backyard shit? Don't you want to see a girl finally dish out the pain?"

She points the knife to the camera. All the phrases, all the genre buzzwords, those are things I've said. She picked them up very quickly, internalized them. Nobody is going to be calling her a fake geek girl.

"I'm Cat Killer and this is what you can expect in my fucking movie," she says, then lowers her voice to address me: "Don't you dare cut that camera."

Anna grabs a clump of Burt's hair, her fingers digging deep enough to get a firm grip on his scalp even with the stocking in the way.

Burt's look of surprise must be a mirror of my own.

Anna bends her legs slightly, straddling Burt and lifting his head over the toilet using both hands, the seat already up. The flat of the knife presses against Burt's forehead as she lifts, she's holding it with two fingers, the others cinched around his hair.

Pressing his clavicle flat against the bowl, she frees her knife hand and leans her knee into him. She's a hooded executioner, her eyes wild.

He's not even fighting, probably because he hasn't seen Rambo, hasn't put it together that this is a real knife.

She cuts Burt's throat and his blood spills into the toilet.

The stream is neat at first, almost too perfect the way it doesn't go anywhere but the bowl, but then she begins sawing and it's everywhere.

When she's done, she's out of breath, and looks at the camera for the first time in over a minute.

"Thanks for watching."

# TEN

When the first slice happens, my immediate thought isn't to scream, isn't to try to help Burt, what I think is: *Damn, that looks good.*

I hate myself for it later.

It is only a second after that—when the knife is already too deep and no one could help Burt—that I feel its realness. Anna going in for her second pass at his neck, in-and-over with the knife, Pez dispensering my oldest friend.

The second emotion to supplant awe, is pants-shitting-terror. Not of Anna, no, my mind still hasn't puzzled out that I'm standing in front of a dangerous person, but I'm scared of the trouble I'm going to be in.

I haven't done anything, but still I have the grade-school end-of-the-world chill. It's the feeling that any second I'm going to be called into the Main Office and, this time, no amount of crying or bargaining is going to stop the principal from calling my house.

*There's no way we can get away with this.* I think, already trying to think of angles, ways to exonerate myself before the blood on the tile has had a chance to cool.

I hold on the scene much longer than I should. Every centimeter of magnetic tape is another year added to my sentence.

39

It's only after I cut the camera that I realize how far Anna's gone and how completely cognizant of her crime she is. This wasn't a heat-of-the-moment mistake, not with the way she followed through like that. She managed to get his head so far off that when she removes her knee the weight of his torso drags his body down but the head refuses to come with it. There's a squeak and a tearing sound that I didn't even know was possible, at least it's never a sound I've heard on film.

We stand in the bathroom and the air around us feels sweaty, like the spilt blood is a heat source, a radiator on full blast. In the silence, I try to work through some possible scenarios. Should I run from her, try for the phone? Am I in a slasher movie now, a possible victim? I'd never make it out the door, I'd trip. I know it.

She's stronger than me, she's proven that, not only a stronger conversationalist, but by nearly beheading my best friend in front of me. Instead of me yelling, screaming or begging, it's her that speaks first. I don't get to ask why, don't panic before she offers an explanation, in a way. In her way.

"You said he lives alone, right?"

I'm silent. *There's no way.*

"Nobody's going to walk in, you can relax. I've just gotten us that five grand."

It's like before, like when I heard her pitch in the staffroom of Stop & Shop.

She talks and I listen, not nodding this time, trying my hardest not to give her much in the way of anything. I don't want her knowing how I'm feeling.

She finishes and I have to admit: it's not a bad plan.

*We can get away with this.*

## ELEVEN

I add a cut to the footage, but not much of one. I use the arrow keys to snip out a few frames before Anna's first knife stroke.

It still looks real, but it no longer looks criminally real.

The idea I'm working from is: when people watch something on a computer screen, they're looking for seams. I've never seen a single viral video that I don't first think was staged.

I delete those few frames, and then once I'm sure that the edited video has been saved in triplicate: I destroy the MiniDV by unspooling it and burning the tape in the sink. I've never done this before, I've never even taped over footage, so I'm surprised by how much black smoke there is, have to fan the fire detector for a good five minutes.

There's now no version of the video that doesn't include that break in reality. It amounts to roughly a quarter of a second, but I think it's enough.

Anything can happen in a quarter of a second, you can cut the camera and replace Burt's neck with a prosthetic, replace Burt's whole body with a meticulously detailed dummy, one that coughs and struggles and drools all over itself as it has its throat cut.

To the community, all Youtube videos are guilty of forgery until proven innocent, and even if they're authentic there's always a vocal contingent that will yell "Fake!" in the comments.

I color balance the scene too, not for cinematic aesthetics, just to make the image a little more processed, throw up more of those "it's gotta be fake" red flags in my audience's mind.

And if the audience is the FBI? Mulder and Scully? Well, by then we're probably fucked anyway, if they're looking. As I see it, that's the weak link in Anna's plan. By the time someone reports him missing, there's a video of where Burt went. She seems most concerned with me cracking up, confessing, but I don't think I will.

What's done is done. And what's done is going to ruin me one way or the other.

When the video's finished I play it through again. It's your normal five minute pledge video until you get to the last minute, and then it's a snuff film.

I'm not going to upload it tonight, I'm going to wait until the morning, watch it again and see how I feel. This is not something to be rushed into.

In the immediate aftermath of the crime, I vomit twice, using Burt's kitchen sink, for obvious reasons. The bathroom is occupied, Burt's lanky frame taking up more space than he ever has, now that he's all over the tile, droplets of him even made it the three feet into the tub.

"We'll come back tonight for the car. And for him," Anna says, motioning to Burt. She's wrapping tape around his body, triple sealing the black plastic garbage bags around his upper torso.

While she does that, I clean the toilet.

I find a cache of cleaning products under the bathroom sink. The stuff hasn't been touched since Burt's mother was alive, but there's a lot of it. The Scrubbing Bubbles smells as chemically strong as ever, maybe even stronger, like it has fermented into ammonia-moonshine.

I get the outside of the bowl too, but I don't do a great job on the first pass and the grout around the base of the toilet turns penny-brown. The stain is a much darker shade than the kind that Caro syrup with red food dye leaves and it serves as one of a million sensory reminders that this has happened.

It's well after eight when we finish cleaning up and is dark by the time we leave. Anna drops me off at my place and then tells me that she'll text me tonight when she's outside.

"Don't fall asleep. I won't call, I'll just text."

There's no indication of how long I'm going to be waiting. I'm not used to this lack of control. Well, maybe I am when you look at my life as a whole, but not in regards to a film.

On set I call the shots, but it's a different business now.

I manage to get the whole video edited together by the time my phone buzzes. It took four hours and it's not an assembly, it's the finished video, color balanced and ready to compress.

I put my hand on top of the PC tower. It's running hot. The external hard drive stays cool enough, though, that's why I bought it. Even though I'm usually a paranoiac that would burn the file to a DVD to be sure, I judge that the backup is safe and hit the button to finalize. A progress bar appears and tells me it'll take about five hours, but it's still estimating, the real time could be less.

I'm just making an uploadable file, not uploading anything. That decision can wait.

Patting my pockets, I make sure that I have my keys and my phone, and then climb the stairs to the first floor.

The upstairs is quiet, my parents are sleeping.

Down the hall in their bedroom, I can hear my father struggle against his uvula. His sleep apnea is louder than I could ever be. Even so, I use my phone as a flashlight, making sure that I don't knock into any furniture on my way out.

The house is carpeted everywhere except for the kitchen, where it's tiled. My tread is near silent, but still I imagine my mother lying awake in bed, sneaking up behind me to ask me where I'm going when it's almost two in the morning.

*She'd turn me in.* We're nowhere near that point yet, only Anna and I know that any kind of crime has been committed, but that's the thought I have anyway. *She would turn her own son in.*

Nothing happens, though. I can see her taillights at the end of the block. I'm out of the house and into the car without incident.

"You don't have a car, but you do have a license, right? I didn't think to ask before." It's the first thing she's said to me in five hours. She's not mechanical or cold, exactly, she's just barely holding it together and putting what's important first. At least, that's how I'm reading her.

Like I said, I'm no good with women.

"I have a license. I can drive." I say, she doesn't look like she buys it though, and can likely tell that I'm trying to convince myself as I say it.

"You'll take my car then," she says.

"Where are we bringing him?"

"I changed my mind, we shouldn't bring him anywhere. It's best if we keep him inside. We're still going to move his car, though. I went to Home Depot after I dropped you off, barely made it before they closed. Then I raided my mother's tool shed. Didn't want to buy too many things at once."

"You live with your parents?"

"Just my mother." She says, and it's like we're on a date, this question no longer restricted to need-to-know information, and I get an answer that tells me more about Anna Friedman, a girl I clearly know nothing about.

I don't ask what she bought at the store, if she used a card or cash. I can guess though, I've seen enough movies and I'm betting that she has too.

She's been delegating the work, giving me the easier stuff. It's not maternal protection and she's not "serving" me, she's being practical, is trying to judge how much I can handle.

That means that I'm the one digging. It's dry work, aside from the sweat, and if I fuck it up it won't land us in prison.

I've always been a pretty skinny guy, never needed to exercise when I was younger and still don't, but now the skin around my midsection has gone soft, curdled up into bumps. I'm not fat, just slack.

I puff as I work through the packed dirt of the basement, clearing out some cardboard boxes and starting to dig in the corner, a few inches away from the foundation. I dig as deep as I can, then move inward towards the middle of the house.

It's easier the deeper I go, until I hit what feels like rock and can't go any further. I scrap this hardened layer as clean as I can, forming a kind of funeral slab.

It's about three and a half feet deep. It may not be the industry-standard six feet, but there's enough room as we heft Burt inside. I carry his legs while Anna takes his arms and plastic-wrapped torso. I check for leaks when we're done and Anna retraces our steps, checking a suspicious spot in the dirt, but it's just a drop of sweat, not blood.

At Home Depot, Anna has purchased a thick blue tarp and three bottles of a drain cleaner called Instant Power Commercial Drain Cleaner. You know it's industrial strength not only by the picture of stainless-steel restaurant equipment on the package, but also because they didn't even bother coming up with a snazzy name for it.

Anna steps into the small hole, swaddling Burt in the tarp as she douses him with drain cleaner. It reeks and I begin to see the smell as a wrinkle in the plan. What if you can smell it from outside? There's only one small basement window, but it's facing the neighbor's house.

"Won't it eat through the tarp, too?" I ask.

"Hopefully not until well after it liquefies him. Even then," she says and taps the end of the shovel against the rock, the metal singing like a tuning fork. I think she's implying that even if it eats through the tarp, he'll still be lying in a kind of concrete trough.

We cover him back up and pat down the dirt. It's not perfect, but you'd only catch it if you were looking for it. I rearrange the cardboard boxes so that the dark, upturned dirt isn't as prominent.

I peel off my thick gardening gloves, but Anna keeps her yellow plastic dish gloves on. I go to set them down and she stops me.

"Give those to me. They're covered in your DNA."

She puts them in the plastic Home Depot bag and ties the handles in a quick knot. I don't ask where those are going, but I probably should, I should probably know everything. Again, I think Anna thinks of me as the largest liability here, so I get nothing, her lips knit so tight that I don't even ask.

"Burt has officially left for vacation," she unknits to deliver a bit more of her script, words she's contrived and now controls.

"Where?" I ask.

"He was a weird guy, he didn't even tell his best friend, didn't give his boss notice."

I make a sound in my closed mouth, kind of an *mhmmm* in the affirmative, it's so casual that it makes me want to sob.

"Let's move his car."

# TWELVE

My eyes should be on the road, but at the first stop light I snoop through as much of Anna's car as I can.

There's a half-eaten cinnamon bagel in the first cup holder, a pack of Kools in the second. I didn't notice the cigarettes this afternoon and haven't seen Anna smoke. I wonder if this is even her car, or whether it's her mother's too. I suddenly want to know more about Anna.

Before today I wanted to know everything, but the list of everything I wanted then was topped by what color panties she was wearing, whether she'd ever date an older guy, one with a gentle dusting of pockmarks on his ass. Now I want to know everything that has the power to help keep me out of trouble, away from the principal's office.

I checked my license back at the house when Anna was out of sight. It expired last January.

Luckily there's no body, no evidence that we're doing anything wrong at all as I crawl behind Burt's car. My foot applies uneven pressure to the gas and every jolt forward gives me a nervous twinge.

It won't be dawn for another two hours, but it still feels more like morning than it does night. I see four a.m. frequently, but I'm never outside for it. Not behind the wheel of a stranger's car.

She signals with Burt's blinkers long before she turns, I don't know where we're heading but it seems like she does.

Like most of the evening up to this point, Anna has more planned out than she's telling me.

I think of the massive, submerged part of an iceberg, then I think of me crashing Anna's early-'90s Lincoln, ripping a chunk out of its side and leaving the engine visible beyond mangled fiberglass and metal.

I clear my mind and focus on my driving.

We pull into the Central Islip train station, a fifteen minute drive from Burt's house. I don't know if Burt's been on the LIRR in his life, but there aren't many people that know much about Burt at all, so I guess it doesn't matter.

There aren't many kids in his neighborhood, more retirees than young families, but if there were kids, Burt would probably be their Boo Radley. A lanky Robert Duvall, too drunk to leave them any presents, so he'd just get all the bad stuff, be that weird guy who lives alone.

Anna parks and I pull in as close as I dare, she only has to walk a few feet to hop in the passenger's side.

"Why here?" I ask and Anna points up to the large fluorescent lamps overlooking the lot. There are holes in some of the posts, wire's hanging out the sides, one has a security camera still attached and the sight of it makes me jump.

"The glass on the front of it is completely busted. I take the train from here. It's a complete ghetto. The local punks sell dimebags and bust out these cameras to keep their weak ass gangs safe."

Holy shit she's thought this out well.

"Gangs?"

"High school kids."

She's right, I don't much consider Long Island to be a hotbed of criminal activity, but thinking about it now I did know a girl from high school who wound up dead in C.I. The bullet caught her in the neck, was meant for her guy, naturally.

I want to pull over, ask her to switch seats with me, but I'm too ashamed. I can see that she's getting ready to talk about what we do next, but I've got too much of my attention on driving to engage her in conversation. It's harder now that I'm not ghosting the movements of a car ahead of me.

We're rolling to stop at a light, there's a 7-11 on the corner and as I look out the driver's window I can see the clerk inside. The guy's got his elbow against the counter. He's either just come in to work or is just about to go off shift. Whatever it is, he looks tired.

"It's green." Anna says.

I hit the gas and she starts talking, there's a feeling so beyond direness in her voice that she's looped back around to a conversational tone.

"I didn't plan it, you know that, right?" she asks.

"I know." I don't really, I just know that she's telling me. Seemed pretty rehearsed to me.

"I'm sorry if this is too much. He was holding you back, he was a sad guy."

It takes me a minute to filter through everything she says and even then I'm not sure I get it all as I'm only half-listening. The feelings I've got going are all over the place.

"You wanted more, you told me that, you told me how tired you were of the same old shit. Me too, it turns out. When I saw him there, it all just came out."

I didn't say anything quite like that. She makes it seem like I was pouring my heart out, crying in my beer over my missed opportunities. It's something I've done, just not something I've done in front of her. I haven't given her anything like this, but still she's smelled it all over me, knows me better than I want her to.

It makes me angry, how much she's guessed, how much she's acted on those guesses, never knowing for sure.

It makes me even angrier that I've gone along with it all, just as she's predicted.

We're done with the feelings portion of the conversation, I don't want to respond to her, probably wouldn't want much to do with her even if she was naked and pouring a glass of Johnny Black.

I stop at the end of my block, ready to walk up to the house rather than risk being seen in this car.

"How does the video look?" she asks.

That's true. She's reminded me that there's still a decision to be made.

## THIRTEEN

I had guessed that it would be an involved process, but nothing like this.

Filling out the Kickstarter page is a nightmare. It could have been worse, though. A few weeks ago, on a whim, drunk, I had used my account to submit a proposal for the new Debaser film. A couple days later I'd gotten an email that the project had been approved, so that's the draft that I'm working from now as I create pledge levels.

I want the rewards to be diverse and enough of a value that people donate, but also want to make sure I can get some money out of the deal.

I'm three quarters of the way done when I get to this section:

*What are the risks and challenges your project may face?*

Oh, if only you knew, Kickstarter.

I type in "Incarceration" and then backspace over it. What I really write is this:

"As with any film project, there are a million things that can go wrong on set, never mind post-production. What counts in this field, though, is one's ability to deal with challenges when they arise. As an experienced team with eight independently produced feature films released (*The*

51

*Debaser, The Debased and the Used, Blood Bubble*), I believe we have the know-how necessary to overcome any challenges. I'm a director that works fast and knows how to properly blend practical and computer effects to get the most out of a scene (as evidenced by our pitch video). I will do my utmost to make sure that pledge rewards are shipped out in a timely matter."

I would no more know how to use a computer to remove Burt's head than I would be able to land the space shuttle, but this answer lets me subtly drop in that yeah: that video is totally fake.

Before hitting the "submit" button, I read everything over one more time, check the spelling and make sure I've got the correct forms on there.

The video is up at the top of the draft, I could watch it again to make sure that it plays correctly on their site, that I've uploaded the correct file, but I know I have so I don't click play, I just send the thing for final approval.

I get a tiny rush as I hit the button, but not much. I don't feel any strong desire to jump into cyberspace after the submission, wrestle it down so nobody can see what we've done. I kinda want them to see, because part of me feels like I'm going down anyway, so that it would be some kind of waste, a slight against Burt's memory even, to not have sent it.

It could go up a few hours from now, a few days, or never. And I could go to prison.

I guess we'll see.

## FOURTEEN

The next day, left without a ride, I'm walking to Stop & Shop. I end up being fifteen minutes late, but I tell myself that's a good thing, that it will help me sell my story a little better.

Deloris watches me clock in and then comes over.

"Everything okay, hon? You're late." She's my boss and my mother, all in one short statement.

"Sorry. I had to walk." I say, and then deliberately move my hand over to Burt's punch card. "Did Burt call in today?" I ask, flicking the corner of the card with only mild concern in my voice. I even try to throw a hint of disappointment, like I'm annoyed that I had to walk, unexpectedly.

"No," she says. Deloris loves me, but isn't too crazy about Burt. This is not the first time he's been late. If he were to come in it wouldn't be the first time he's come in still drunk.

But he's not coming.

"He didn't answer my texts," I say and shrug. "Weird." I plan to leave it here, this is enough for now. Tomorrow's Saturday and neither of us are on the schedule, so I won't have to put on another show until Monday morning.

I'm behind my register and ringing in an elderly lady, an early shopper, before I remember that I should have checked the schedule to see when Anna works, if she's on today.

"Six seventy-five," I say to the lady, she's familiar, one of the shriveled biddies that populates the store on weekday mornings. "Would you like me to double bag this?"

She looks up at me, confused, like her world has been upended. Her eyes are close to teary, the way old people eyes seem to be perpetually. "Did you run a card for me?" she asks.

"I'm sorry about that, ma'am," I say and throw my laminated UPC across the beam. The card knocks a whole fifteen cents off the lady's cream of wheat.

"Yes, double bag it, please," she says, her boring life has been reset on its rails, a turtle picked up off its shell and placed right-way so that her feet touch the ground.

Anna doesn't show up until after lunch and by then I've forgotten to run a Super Saver card for at least a dozen customers.

"And?" she asks. She's leaning over my register, all smiles. One customer sees her, then decides it would be best to move to a different lane.

"And what?" I don't know how she can be so cool.

"Is it up yet? Are we making a movie or what?" She reaches over and touches my arm. For bystanders the touch probably looks like flirting, but I get the message she's sending: *relax, don't ruin this when we're so close.*

Looking down, I notice that the cut on her arm has been neatly bandaged, the only evidence that she's been injured a pale square band-aid, so similar in tone to her flesh that I have to struggle to remember if she had it on last night or not. She probably did, wouldn't allow the possibility of leaving a drop of her own blood in Burt's car.

"I submitted it for approval. We should know soon."

"I thought you said you did that already?" Her voice is sugary sweet and she's got her polo unbuttoned much lower than regulation, but I'm in no mood.

"The first time, for the proposal. It still takes a little while." It will take even less time for me than it does other first-timers, because I've already got in Amazon Payments account in semi-good standing. I could elaborate about this, but I don't. Fuck her.

"Deloris mentioned that you may need a ride after work today. Is that true?"

I force myself to smile, because it's the only thing that stops me from revving up the conveyor belt and feeding her American Girl ponytail into the gears.

"I'll drive you home on my break," she says. "See you later."

In the car she's different, less chipper, but there's still a smile.

I check the cup holder and the Kools are gone, somehow this seems important, but it's not really, doesn't change much of anything. The cinnamon bagel is still there, though, hard as a rock.

"You can't be a wreck. What happened to the badass that cuts up girls in his spare time?" She'd make a good high school football coach.

I stare out the window.

"You haven't tweeted since yesterday afternoon. Don't change your routine."

I hadn't thought of that. She's right. I wonder what @ Cat_Killer's been saying since last night, wonder how many followers she has now.

Her hand finds my thigh, the five inch stretch above my knee, and rubs until a patch of my jeans are warm.

"I was looking online, have you ever been to the Chiller Theatre convention?"

I have. It's wonderful. It's next weekend. I have two tickets already, bought them months ago.

"It's next weekend, the eighteenth? I figured we could go and hand out fliers. I could be in costume."

"They have it twice a year, Burt and I go." It's a horror convention, like a comic book con with less (but still some) storm troopers.

"I can drive us. It's not a long drive, not far into New Jersey."

I don't say yes or no, but I know that if we're not in police custody, that's where we'll be. Changing the subject, I bring up something I've been thinking about.

"Burt's father has a key to the house."

She tightens her grip on the wheel, I'm annoying her. "So?"

"He might stop in if he doesn't hear from his son. Did we clean well enough?" Or *too* well, I get a strong sense memory of the smell of the late-90s bottle of Scrubbing Bubbles.

Her hand on my thigh creeps up, to the point where I think it may be going all the way, but then she diverts and grabs my hand.

We're at the end of my block now and she pulls the car to the corner and stops.

She shakes my hand until I make eye contact with her, demanding that I listen.

"He's not going to check. Even if he did, a million to one chance, he's not going to find anything. You need to relax. They'll tow his car. His father won't check. You said that they don't speak."

I said that I don't *think* that they speak *much*, but there's that think word again.

She takes two of my fingers and presses them down the top of her panties. She's warm, but not as warm as one would hope. I don't want this and don't understand why I'm getting it.

It's daylight, but no one is on the streets.

"Things are going to," she says, pausing and exhaling as she pushes my fingers down, moving them for me, "be fine."

We sit there for another moment, me a passive party in this sex act. She's choked up on my fingers, just moving the tips. Her breathing is heavy, but not exaggerated. I buy it.

When it sounds like she's done, or getting there, I curl my fingers in and catch her softness with one of my fingernails, hopefully leaving a cut.

"Shit," she says.

"Sorry," I say and push out of the car.

My hand drying and my thigh cooling, I walk my street. I don't know the names of anyone on my block with the exception of the neighbor we share a fence with. Small town façade, big city anonymity. Burt's block is the same. A bunch of old people, ready to crump. Nobody's going to miss him.

Except maybe the cable company, but they won't send the cops. Will they? Not this soon, surely?

## FIFTEEN

I've got my clothes folded and laid over a towel. I put my hand on the bathroom doorknob, but it opens before I can touch it.

"Nicky," my mother says, surprised to see me on my way to shower in the daytime, I guess.

"Hi ma, do you need the bathroom?"

"Are you okay? You look sick." Her hand is on my face before I can smack it away, but her interest in my well-being is momentary. "How is that girl, uh, Anna?" She tries to make it sound like she'd had trouble remembering Anna's name, but that's unlikely, the two of them spent yesterday gabbing. Anna must have left a good impression, I wonder if I should bring up the pictures I have on my phone, maybe give her a whiff of my fingers.

"You like her, Nicky?" My mother's five-six, two hundred pound frame is two seconds from doing a standing-somersault. That's how excited she is. I don't think I've seen her this happy since Nicholas was in the business of making macaroni pictures.

"She's good, ma," I say ignoring the second question. "Can I shower?" She's body-blocking the bathroom. This is why I usually wait until after midnight to shower, when I shower.

"Sure, sure," she moves out of the way, her hand on my shoulder before I pass. "You be good to her, Nicholas, she's good for you."

"Yeah mom." I shut myself in the bathroom and steam up the hot water, to see if I can burn some of the dirt off.

The shower makes my sore muscles feel better when the water is falling, but as I towel myself off and cool, my joints harden, like concrete setting.

As my hair dries, I sit at my desk and I send out a few tweets. Most of them are links to my movies on Amazon. When I'm not in the mood, I self-promote, it may be lazy but the posts write themselves.

"How much sick shit can you take? THE DEBASER wants to find out! #indie #horror #gore http://amzn.to/1b8cGZZ"

I fall asleep while the sun is still peeking through the gaps in the tin foil I use to cover the basement windows. Reynolds wrap makes cheap blackout shades.

I'm awoken by the buzz of a text, then another in rapid succession.

"It's up"

"The Kickstarter"

It's three in the morning. Has Anna slept at all? I imagine her manically refreshing the page, hitting the search button. It's something I would have done, too. If I weren't so sore from digging graves, so sick to my stomach.

I don't respond to the text, and instead hold the button on top of my phone and power it off completely. My alarm isn't set because tomorrow's a day off, so I have nothing to risk beyond snubbing Anna. It may not be the best decision, I've seen what she's capable of, but I need my beauty rest.

I let sleep pull me back under.

## SIXTEEN

I can't remember the last time there's been a knock on my door. That's not true, I can remember, but it was months ago, my mother had intercepted a package of Japanese gore porn and insisted on questioning me about it. That had been a Saturday too.

"Nicky!" I can hear my mother's voice through the door. She's at the top of the stairs, but her voice carries down the hallway, is amplified like an echo chamber as it bounces around the cinderblock walls of the basement.

She calls my name again as I stretch, rub the gunk out of my eyes. When I hear her the second time, I realize that she's calling me Nicky instead of Nicholas. If she were pissed, had been opening my mail again, she would be calling for Nicholas.

"Your friend is here," she says.

I'm pulling on pants and for a loopy dream-second I think she means Burt.

I pick a t-shirt up off the floor and pull it on. The shirt's a limited edition Fright Rags. I probably shouldn't be wearing it so many times in a row without washing it, but running it through the machine degrades the print, even when you set the water temperature to cold and let it drip dry.

I take the steps two at a time and am winded as I confirm what I've feared. Anna's standing in my living room. She's smiling, of course, but my mother's there, so I expect that. She's done up in her Anna Friedman costume, hair pulled back in a conservative ponytail. It takes all the attention away from her highlights and makes her wholesome, like she's captain of the high school field hockey team, all-state.

"Have a nice sleep?" she asks.

"You sleep the day away, Nicky. It's no good." My mother chimes in, pumping up the Greek mother routine, an accent appearing like magic.

Great, I've got them in stereo now.

Last night, when I got the text, I imagined Anna sitting by her laptop, maybe Indian-style on the floor, her face sallow and vertebra poking up from her curved back. A cross between Gollum and the girl in *Audition*, but now her eyes are fresh, no bags, and he hair looks recently washed and primped. She looks great. There's the Anna I imagine and the Anna that the world sees, I wonder which one's closer to the truth.

"See my texts?" she asks. "I tried calling but it went straight to voicemail."

My mother's still standing there, a third party in the conversation. I wave her away, but she stays put.

"Yeah, sorry, I had my phone off." I look around, then duck my head under the partition between the living room and kitchen to check the clock on the microwave. The clock reads a few minutes to two. I've been asleep for nearly twenty hours. That's almost a new record.

"The page is up!" She's bubbly, she's making an announcement and my mother's catching the bug and puts a hand on Anna's shoulder. Who knows how long they were up here talking before my mother knocked on the basement door. Anna's here for the long haul, has inserted herself into my family.

I do a little math, remembering when the text was last night. That means that we're at least eleven hours into our thirty day campaign. I can't help it, I'm curious to see if anyone's pledged yet.

"Has anyone, you know?" I say.

"You really haven't looked at it?" she asks, then looks at my mother who rolls her eyes. My mother can't check her email without my help, so I doubt that she grasps what it is we're talking about.

I open up the basement door and motion for Anna to follow me.

"Excuse us, Mrs. Anastos."

"So polite," my mother says, practically swooning. "She's so polite, Nicky." It's like she's listing the features of an appliance, *she slices* and *dices*.

Anna follows me downstairs and I begin to boot up my computer.

This is the first time Anna's been down here without me cleaning up first. A quick shadow of disgust passes across her face, but she stifles it. If this grosses her out, she should see it when I've had a chance to stink it up, really pile up the pizza boxes and spent tissues.

"You don't work today?" I ask, not much concerned that I won't be making the cover of *Good Housekeeping* this month.

"I'm on break," she says. "You can't turn your phone off like that. We need to be able to reach each other."

Ignoring the fact that I'm being dressed down, I bring up Firefox and begin to search for our project.

"You don't need to type it in," she says. "Scroll down to the film category." She leans over me, her finger rolling the wheel while I've still got my hand gripping the small, portable laser mouse.

Then I see it, our thumbnail: Rambo, slick with blood, the words *The Debaser Vs. Cat Killer* superimposed over the image. It's a screencap that I took from the video itself, the words added with a bootleg copy of Photoshop.

We're featured under the Staff Picks section, right at the top of the page. More than that, our progress bar, the green line that I've anticipated would be charting our slow failure, is more than halfway there.

"No fucking way." I say. There's surprise in me, of course, but there's joy too.

She clicks, her fingers pressing mine on the mouse. I'm reminded of our hook up in the car, pressing her button. I wasn't turned on then, but I am now.

Sixty-two backers, $2,631.

She turns to me. It's the first time I've gotten a real, private smile, one that wasn't also for the onlookers at Stop & Shop or my mother, since we made the tape.

"How?" I ask. It sure as shit wasn't our stellar sound design.

"I sent some emails last night and this morning. Here, check out Dread and Bloody."

She opens two tabs, scrolling down through the day's news to find our thumbnail somewhere on both front pages.

"Our twitter accounts are blowing up too. I even dropped it on those forums you showed me, hope you don't mind."

I kiss her. It's the first first kiss I've ever initiated. It's just a peck, then I'm back to reading the coverage.

Brad Miska gives me the best backhanded compliment I've ever received: "Be warned the attached pledge video is NSFW: schlockmeister Anastos has clearly learned a thing or two between his last bottom feeder of a film, because this video features some of the roughest violence we've seen in a long while."

Anna wraps her arms around my neck and I can feel her breasts pressing against my back. I have to push images of Burt's death from my mind, but it's easier now than it was when I was going to sleep.

"I guess we have to start working on the film now," she whispers in my ear. Her breath is warm now, much warmer than any part of her was in the car.

I turn in my seat and she plants a kiss on me. Not a peck. She begins to show me how it's done.

"Shouldn't you get back to work?" I ask, "Maintaining our normal routines and all that?"

"I'm thinking of quitting and taking up acting full time." She pulls me to her.

I don't even think that she closed the basement door behind her. It doesn't matter. I don't care. Let them listen.

When we're finished I check the page again and we've raised another three hundred dollars.

## SEVENTEEN

"We've got an interview request." Anna says, scrolling through her phone, standing in my checkout aisle. She's been told by Deloris to put the phone in her locker, but she doesn't.

I like Deloris, wish that Anna would listen to her, but it's no use arguing.

By the fourth day of the campaign, pledges have slowed considerably, but we're already funded and are closing in on six grand. I've added High Definition as a stretch goal and I'm already looking into renting the Red Scarlet camera. I'll have to upgrade my computer as well, but I think we'll have the money.

"Who wants to talk to us?" I ask.

"Some guy with a blog," she says, scrolling with her thumb. "Looks like shit."

"How many followers on twitter?"

"Seven hundred."

"Tell him we'll get back to him." We probably won't, this guy's clearly small potatoes. Besides, things are about to get very busy for me. Last night I ordered some plaster and latex, along with some how-to books that I've had my eyes on for a while. I've worked with this stuff a little bit in the past, but now I get to really try, I've got Rockefeller cash.

Anna's still clicking on the phone when a customer pushes a cart up behind her.

"I can take you, sir." I say and wave Anna out of the way.

My mouth goes dry when I recognize him.

He's got a few rolls of paper towels and a stack of Hungry Man dinners in his cart, but I don't think that's why he drove all the way out to Stop & Shop when Pathmark is way closer for him.

"Hello Tony. Is Burt around?" Burt's dad says. His voice is a wheeze, emphysema or something. I didn't recognize him at first because his face is so different from the last time I saw him, that was maybe three years ago. He's lost weight. A lot of weight.

Anna's at the end of the aisle, has begun opening a plastic bag, her phone back in her pocket and all attention on this exchange. As far as I know, she's never been on bag duty in her life. We have a mentally challenged guy on staff that usually helps with that, otherwise some cashiers will do it themselves. I usually only help feeble looking customers.

My mouth is dry, my tongue feels heavy, like it has swollen and is about to choke me to death, but then I speak.

"Mr. Ernst, is that you?" I say, trying to put on a tone of happy surprise, hoping my voice doesn't crack. "I haven't seen you in forever."

I begin to ring in Hungry Mans, a sudden need to keep my hands occupied. Anna stuffs them into bags longways, the corners already straining against the package. She doesn't double bag.

"I checked the produce section. I can't seem to find my son." The skin of his face wrinkles as he talks, it's like crepe paper, I imagine it tearing if he opens his mouth too wide. The sound I lay over this image is Burt's neck stretching, squeaking against the toilet.

What few interactions I've had with Burt's dad usually involved him telling me corny jokes. I can't remember any of them now, I know one punchline has a guy pointing at his brains and saying "Kidneys." It was funny then, but he's not joking now.

"That's weird, because I haven't heard from him either. I think he's running out of sick days."

"His car isn't in his driveway."

I swallow hard. He's been at the house but has he been inside? Has he smelled anything off? Has he gone down to the basement?

"Huh. He usually drives me to work, but I couldn't get ahold of him on Friday," I say. I'm done with the groceries now, but haven't told him his total yet. "Is he in the city maybe?" It's a stupid thing to say, but I don't want any silences, don't want his red eyes on me without one of us talking.

"Does he go, usually?" Mr. Ernst asks.

No, but this will help explain why his car shows up at the train station, if it hasn't been towed already. My answer is either smooth or incriminating.

Anna finishes dropping the last roll of toilet paper in the bag, then drops it onto the counter and moves out of sight, deeper into the store. She's left me to it. I don't know if this is a vote of confidence or if she's skipping to Mexico.

"I don't know. Not that I know of. When he didn't answer my texts I thought he was mad at me, or sick. He gets moody sometimes. I guess I don't need to tell you that."

"Yeah," he says and hands me his debit card without hearing the total.

"Do you have a Super Saver card?" I ask, grateful for the routine of the words.

He doesn't, but I run one for him anyway. Then I take his phone number down on a bit of paper from the receipt roll. I'll call him if I hear anything.

## EIGHTEEN

It's Wednesday night and I've got Anna's face wrapped up like a mummy. It's the only peace I've had all day: she can't talk.

Not that she has been talking much, but without the wet plaster over her mouth, there's now not even the threat of her saying anything. That's what's been tying me in knots, the thought of her saying aloud some of the things that I've been thinking, externalizing them into a conversation I can't ignore.

*He hasn't filed a missing persons. Yet.*

The first stage is coating her face in casting alginate, leaving everything but her nostrils covered. Now I lay down the last strips of plaster. This stuff is top shelf, but I still have to use it right to get the most out of my money, so I've overloaded Anna's face with plaster.

The water I'm using to moisten the strips started out warm but is now room temperature. I could go upstairs and get more from the sink, but I don't think it much affects the outcome of the plaster cast. I keep laying it on. Anna's probably getting a little cold, but fuck her.

She *should* be a little uncomfortable. I am, as the thoughts keep rising up in my mind.

*Do you think he has friends? Belongs to a bowling league or something? Do you think he's seen a doctor about that wheeze? Does he have appointments? Will he be missed?*

"That's the last one. Now we wait twenty minutes," I say. The how-to video I watched said to wait ten minutes, but I want to be extra sure. Plus it's ten more minutes we don't have to talk.

Anna gives me a thumbs up.

I'm making the lifecast, but it has no specific use in the movie, yet. It's just something to experiment with and Anna's the only actor we've brought on so far. I don't feel up to holding casting calls yet. If the script winds up calling for facial prosthetics, I can use this cast of Anna's face to prepare them, making sure they fit exactly.

"How about some music?"

Another thumbs up.

I put on the *Re-Animator* soundtrack. It's a shameless borrowing of the *Psycho* score, but fun in its own way. I feel a bit of remorse for downloading it illegally, but people steal my movies all the time, so I know that I'm owed.

Anna sits still in her chair and I click around on the computer. There's one browser tab that I plan on keeping open for the rest of my life, I try to resist the urge to check it first thing, but I just peek. We're up another five hundred since I've gotten home from work. Anna drove me, has spent every night this week here.

I still wonder about those Kools, because the car's been parked in our driveway for the past three nights. It doesn't seem like Anna shares it with her mother. I haven't asked. I don't talk to her about anything but the film and even that is in the sketchiest of terms. I have plot ideas, but I don't share them, I don't want to cede any more control than I already have.

What little extra personal information about Anna I've gathered has been from dinner.

Earlier, as we're sneaking down to my room, my mother catches us and insists we join my parents for dinner. Before Anna arrived on the scene, I'd take a plate down to my room or raid the fridge late at night. I haven't shared a meal with my parents since high school.

At least part of what she tells my mother are lies, but I'm not sure how much.

"How did you meet?"

"We work together at the grocery store."

"Where are your parents from?"

"The city. The Bronx."

"Do you like scary movies like my son?"

"Of course. Who doesn't?"

"Me. How old are you, do you mind me asking?"

"Not at all. I'm twenty."

I don't field any of the questions, but it's okay because none of them are directed at me. I only get one statement tossed my way, toward the end of the night, when Anna's said something mildly charming and gotten both my parents laughing.

My mother leans over to me, loud enough for everyone to hear, and asks: "Isn't it so much nicer to spend time with Anna instead of that terrible pervert?"

She means Burt and, yeah, I guess it is.


"Don't move your head, just keep perfectly still and I'll do all the work."

If Burt was here, he'd be chiming in with a "that's what she said." Never thought I'd miss that. Still don't, not really.

I pull the plaster off first. It's soft in spots, maybe because I made too thick a layer. It sticks to the alginate in several places and leaves divots big enough that I'm worried they'll become holes when I remove the alginate from Anna's skin.

I use my fingernails to work a flap of the fleshy alginate off of her neck, and then lift up, like I'm helping her to take off a very snug mask.

The mold is perfect, so much better than the time Burt and I had tried to do it with the cheaper stuff. Then our actress had been unable to keep still and had refused to wash off her makeup beforehand. That mold had been filled with bubbles and inconsistencies.

I hold the mask up to the light. There's just the slightest hint of color in Anna's alginate lips, some light pink residue left by the lipstick that didn't come off on the tissue.

Despite the mold's greenish skin, these pink lips give the cast a lifelike quality, as if it were about to open those lips and ask me something.

"Do you think we have to do something about Burt's father?" the real Anna asks, interrupting my thoughts.

"He's not going to go through the trouble. You saw him, heard him. It was difficult for him to travel out to Stop & Shop, he's not going to continue his investigation. They didn't get along, not really."

"So he'd let his only child just vanish? He would believe that Burt could just leave like that?"

"Yeah," I say, but it doesn't seem that she likes that answer.

## NINETEEN

The next day we don't go on break or eat lunch together. It's not that I don't want to, I assumed that we were going to, but when I'm ready to head out I can't find her. She's not in the breakroom and the employee restroom has the door left open, unoccupied.

I walk out into the parking lot, finishing a miniature bag of M&Ms I've taken from a package that I caught some kids opening without paying for.

The car (hers, her mother's, whoever's) is not there.

Suddenly I'm thinking of where we left our situation last night. My balls crawl up into my body, a gym class race to the top of the rope.

I sit on the stoop outside, thinking it over, wishing I had more M&Ms.

*I didn't tell her where he lives.*

*But she's clever. I'm sure she can use the internet, idiot. Everyone's address is online, she could use Google Maps to pick his specific apartment out from space.*

Twenty-five minutes later, when I'm just about to go back inside, the car pulls in.

It's a big parking lot, part of a strip mall, so Anna's just a speck in the distance as she exits the driver's side. I can see that she's carrying something, though.

I ask myself how long she could have possibly been gone, it's hard to remember the last time I saw her today. I'm guessing that the maximum is an hour. She had time to make it to Lindenhurst and back, but not for much else.

I have flashes of Mr. Ernst at the bottom of a flight of stairs, his head turned the wrong way, or lying in bed, a bruise at the bridge of his nose where a pillow has been mashed.

Standing, I start walking out into the lot, closing the distance between us. There are people around, pushing carts or driving slow, gunning for spots.

"Where were you?" I shout more than I want to.

She lifts an eyebrow, giving me that quizzical little girl face. Asking "What do you mean?" while she's got her hand in the cookie jar up to the elbow. She's holding a small square box in front of her.

"I was going to hang them up on the bulletin board to surprise you, but I guess you caught me."

She opens the lid and hands me a bright-green flier and I read it.

"Help us Kickstart the film they didn't want you to see!"

Under that is one of the snaps of Anna in costume, legs spread wide in the torn stockings, Rambo covering her snatch. At the bottom is our information.

I don't remember taking this picture. I try to remember back to that night, what Anna did with the murder weapon, but I can't. All I can remember is scrubbing porcelain.

"I've got another two boxes in the car. We can wallpaper the convention with them."

"You just went and these made yourself? Right now?" I ask. I'm not concerned that she went out of pocket on them, I'm still trying to account for her whereabouts. "Staples does stuff like this, you know."

I point to the far end of the strip mall, to the Staples.

"I had them done at that place on Main. Shop local, ya know," she takes the flier from me and stacks it neatly back on top of the box and replaces the lid.

"You don't like them?" she asks. "The other boxes are printed on different colors."

"They're great. Really." I shake my head from side to

side, trying to look like I'm snapping out of a daze. "Sorry, I just didn't know where you went. I thought we were getting lunch."

"I've got some yogurt in the fridge. Reese's mix-ins."

We begin to walk back towards the store and I offer to take the box from her. There's a thick stack of freshly made photocopies inside, but the bottom of the box is cool to the touch.


"We've been seeing a lot of each other. It's not bad, but it's not exactly sticking to a routine." That's how I keep her out of my house when she drops me off.

It works, she drives off eventually. But I can see something in the back of her eyes when I say the words. I hear Robert Shaw. *Black eyes. Like a doll's eyes.*

When I'm inside the knot that has cinched tight around my heart and lungs unravels and I can breathe again. I thought it would be worse, not having Anna there, but she keeps me strung up, careful what I say and do. In my room I can finally do what I want, be myself.

First thing I do is have a drink.

There's only one bottle in my room and it's from back when I used to hide these kinds of things from my parents, buried under a pile of laundry in my closet. I take a slug of the old bottle. Fireball whiskey, disgusting shit that tastes like sugar and cinnamon. Warm, it's even worse.

I can't even do a second sip. It's okay, because drinking only makes me think of Burt anyway. If the bottle was Vodka I'd probably be sobbing into it, dialing up my local precinct.

I put the bottle down and check the Kickstarter. I've got it on the browser of my phone now, so I bring it up on the small screen even though my computer is a foot away and powered up.

We're beyond ten grand now, another stretch goal met. Every contributor of fifty bucks or more gets a limited t-shirt. Now I've got to look into getting someone to design that.

That's the total already and we've got over three weeks left to go.

Anna got us the money. So much money that the thought of being found out through the video doesn't worry me anymore. Thousands of people have watched the pitch, and none of those views has resulted in the admins pulling the project. Or a visit from the police.

What I'm really concerned with is Burt's dad, if he's breathing or not.

Walking two towns over to check on the old man isn't an option and neither is hanging around Burt's house after sundown to see if anyone's been inside.

We leave for Chiller Theatre, for East Rutherford, New Jersey, tomorrow straight from work. Anna says she even plans on switching into her Cat Killer costume in the staff bathroom. If Deloris wants to fire her for her excessive "swag", she claims that's no problem.

I pace the basement, alone for the first time in days but pent in all the same. From my desk, the cast of Anna's face looks at me, even with its eyes sealed shut.

I need a real drink.

My parents used to measure the bottles in the liquor cabinet, mark them off and date them with green Sharpie. It doesn't surprise me to see that they still do. The most recent date, on a bottle of Beefeater, is Monday. I don't even like gin, but something about the fresh green line of permanent marker makes me want something floral.

Not waiting until I get downstairs, I grab a glass and fill it. The smell seems strong enough to wake my parents even if the clanging of glass isn't.

My father walks out of the hallway and grunts at me.

"I'll buy you another bottle. Cool your jets." I say, turn and begin to descend the stairs.

"Wait." He says. An actual, full word. Directed at me. Interesting.

I poke my head through the doorframe and he waves me towards him, walks to the liquor cabinet himself and takes a glass. He blows into it, the dust going straight into his eyes but he tries not to show that he's just pained himself.

"Fill'er up."

I do. And we drink.

It's not like I don't see my dad. I run into him almost every day, but we never talk. Even at the dinner table last night he was silent, nodding along to some of the things Anna was saying, laughing at the appropriate times. He keeps his eyes on me now.

"That's a good girl you got. Better than you'd think. Looking at you, you being like you are."

He smiles, this is as close to a compliment as I've received since I quit peewee soccer at age nine. We could stand here and finish our drink in peace if that was where he leaves it. But it's not.

"What's wrong with her?" he asks.

It's not a set up to a joke, it's a question. I fill my glass to the brim and replace the bottle in the cabinet. As I turn the question over I feel a warmth inside that isn't just the liquor hitting me.

"Nothing's wrong with her. She's perfect, didn't you see?" I think of her perfection, her lips and ass and wonder where she is tonight. I imagine her mother, what I imagine she looks like, standing by the sink smoking a Kool and asking her daughter where she's been spending all her time.

The image of Anna and her mother is detailed: her mom knocking ash into the stainless steel of the sink and then running the tap. But it's just an image, artful lying. I don't know where Anna is right now.


It's two a.m. and I've already been upstairs once to refill. Not gin this time, gin had been a bad idea, almost as gross as the Fireball.

A few days without drinking and I feel like my tolerance has taken a hit, the room is bubbly.

My confidence is at an all time high, though, so I take out the latex solution I ordered online and begin to brush it onto the mold. I forget to plug up her nostrils and the goop is dripping down my hand as I apply it as evenly as I can across the mold.

When I'm sure there are not missed spots, I place the alginate mold on the desk and look to the boxes at my feet.

I haven't broken the packaging on half of the crap I've ordered, so I do now. I lay out all the paints, gels and putties, most of which I have never used or have any idea how, then I open up a small canvas bag with all my new sculpting tools.

There's one that looks like a surgeon's scalpel and I take it out and test it against my finger. Even buzzed, I'm not a badass like Anna, so I stop well short of when it feels like I might break the skin.

I glance at the clock on the desktop, it's only been three minutes and the latex isn't ready yet. The layer that I've spilt on my hand is good and tacky, though, so I start carving that off.

When I've got a lip free with the knife I pull with my other hand and watch my own skin stretch away. My fingerprints are prominent, even in the crappy light of the basement.

Without checking the clock again, feeling that surely it must be done, I begin to peel Anna's latex face out of the mold. It's sticking though, because I've forgotten to dust the inside with baby powder. Rookie mistake.

The latex copy is not only stretched and disfigured, but I've torn the alginate too.

I sit back in the chair, a mixture of gin, vodka and Fireball bubbling up in my throat. I've got a ruined face in each hand as I fall asleep. B,oth of them don't look as if they like me much.

## TWENTY

Anna kicks the chair to wake me.

I jolt upright like I'm falling, dropping the mold to the floor where it bounces, Anna's face folding inwards and then recoiling like Jell-O.

"Were you going to sleep through the convention?" she asks, inspecting the mess around me. Passing out last night, I thought it would be worse. There's not nearly as much dried latex as I remember spilling, though the paintbrush is ruined, its bristles now one solid mass. It's okay, I have more.

"Have you even packed?"

I forgot that we're going to stay the night, it'll be the first time that Chiller Theatre hasn't been a day trip. Sharing a hotel room with Burt always seemed kinda intimate, so we never spent the extra cash.

I check the time on my phone, smearing it with dirty fingerprints. I've slept past work and it's time to leave for the show. That's one way to cut down on the pre-con anxiety I usually feel.

I toss a shirt and a pair of underwear into a backpack as Anna inspects her ruined faces.

"You're going to get better at this, right?" she asks, holding up the alginate mold, pulling at the tears. "This kind of work isn't going to make me a star."

I don't blame it on being drunk, though she must smell it on me, must know. She's just fucking with me.

"Turn around, I'm going to change," she says, her voice trying to start something.

"I'll let you have your privacy," I say, zipping up my bag. "I'll meet you outside."

I take the stairs two at a time, fleeing the basement before I can see whatever expression I've just caused, be it sadness, rage or something else.


In the car she has none of the steely cool, the pent up manic energy that that she exhibited in the twenty-four hours after Burt's death.

I judge this as a good sign, let myself relax a little. Maybe nothing has happened to Mr. Ernst, maybe I'm just too nervous for my own good. Or maybe she's just getting better at killing, doesn't let it rattle her any more. Or maybe her being rattled was a show for me.

I try to push the thoughts away. I'm not a criminal psychologist, though, no matter how many documentaries about Ed Gein I've seen.

"Do you go to these things and get recognized?" she asks. "Do people know you?"

"Yeah, some. We used to buy vendor space to sell our movies, but we've stopped in the last few years, not worth it."

"That's so cool." She says, her enthusiasm not really linking up with what I've just said. "Do you think I'll get recognized?"

There's her real question.

"The amount of coverage we've got, I'm sure you will."

She smiles and uses one hand to readjust her tanktop. It's the happiest I've ever seen her, pre- or post-murder. If we get pulled over for speeding, there's not a cop in the world that would give her a ticket, her looking as hot as she does.

"You've never been to one of these things, though. So

you should prepare yourself for disappointment, it may not be like you think it is. The people can get weird."

She doesn't seem to hear this, though, then leans over and turns up the radio to drown out the truth, before I speak again.

We make it to the hotel in record time, Anna driving in-character, with Cat Killer's speed and recklessness.

## TWENTY-ONE

We drop off our bags in the room and Anna is recognized three times before we get down to the show floor. All three of the guys asks to take a picture with her, each of them asks me if I can hold the camera.

Anna tells them thanks, stuffs a flier into each of their sweaty hands. She doesn't mind being pawed by these guys, guys that are way bigger creatures than me.

We get down to the dealers room, where it smells like a farm and the aisles are so packed that it's difficult to turn around, and she's stormed. Neckbeards and foodstains and utilikilts, Anna never flinches, she takes all comers, wrapping both arms around them and pressing her cheek close for a photo.

Maybe one in ten of them knows who I am and acknowledges me.

I wander away from the minor scene she's causing, am contented by the fact that she's still handing out fliers, reminding everyone that she talks to that if they haven't pledged they really should and if they have they should look at some of our deluxe pledge tiers. We'll probably double our money in one day.

The dealer room has only gotten more impressive in the years I've been coming to this thing, but even though it has

81

swollen, it's lost some of its luster for me. I used to be so excited to browse the bootleg discs, all out of print stuff or VHS dupes that you couldn't find anywhere. But now most of it can be searched up on Youtube, consumed in ten minute chunks.

I look down at a spread of knives and swords. The dealer recognizes me and comes over. "Hey, how've you been?" he says. I'm just a face to him, a mark, he doesn't know my name. He's wearing sunglasses inside, has his head shaved bald. It's 2013 and he's still rocking the look that Joe Pantoliano wore in *The Matrix*. I never realized how sad that was until right now.

"I'm okay. I'm here with my movie, we've raised over ten grand in our first week."

"Wow that's great, I remember you coming here forever. See anything you like?"

I don't want any knives.

"Hey, don't leave me alone like that. I was getting swamped," Anna says as she pokes me in the ribs, scares me.

"You don't like it?"

"Oh it's great. Most of them are great."

"Most?" I say, picking up an item from the table, one of the boomerangs from the movie *Blade*. I don't feel like dealing with Anna, so I wonder what Wesley Snipes is up to, whether he's sunken low enough to start working on low budget Kickstarter features.

"Yeah, there's this one guy that keeps hanging around, staring at my ass." That doesn't narrow it down, most of this aisle is staring at her ass, the knife dealer is staring at her ass, even the girls are staring. Her ass is apparent, it commands attention, especially since we can see most of it.

"Which one?" I ask, looking around, not much caring.

"The fat one," she says. Again, really slimming down the candidates. "The one with the Freddy glove."

I see him now, he's looking but trying to look like he's not. The way his eyes are going crazy in their sockets I suspect that there's something wrong with him, like more than there is wrong with all the other people that have paid fifty dollars to have c-list celebrities charge them for autographs. There are a good amount of special folks who frequent these conventions, from crippling social anxiety to autism to full blown shrapnel damage. I used to get a kick out of seeing how the celebrities would interact with these people. If they were dicks, things could get sad.

"He's a feeb, don't let him bother you," I say, then turn my attention to the guy. "She doesn't like you staring at her, go away before I kick your ass." The guy scatters, a few rubberneckers look at me, some of them laugh.

"Excuse me, can you take a picture?" a guy says and presses his phone into my hands, grabbing onto Anna by the shoulder, she's not having it and neither am I.

"Ask first, asshole." I say. I'm a quiet guy, don't usually talk like that to strangers, even when they do deserve it.

"I just wanted a picture," he plucks his phone back from me, "no reason to be a dick."

Anna has regained her sexed-up composure and is still trying to hand him a flier as he walks away.

She turns back to me, "I need to go up to the room and take a break."

There's a pause, I say okay, that I'm going to keep looking down here, that I'll see her when she's back. This really pisses her off and for the first time since we've arrived I'm happy. She starts walking away, cutting through the crowd and I watch as the Freddy glove guy peels off, starts following her.

I'm not going to babysit her, but I do send her a text, it's the responsible thing:

"Be safe. Don't let your secret admirer follow you up to the room."

A few minutes later, sifting through some old Aurora model kits, I get a text that reads "I can handle myself."

## TWENTY-TWO

I'm not where I say I'm going to be. After looking through the dealer room, too empty to buy anything, I head for the hotel bar, the best part of the convention.

The beers are seven bucks apiece, but it's worth it for the atmosphere. I've seen some crazy shit at this bar, seen character actors recite lines of dialogue from movies that are twenty years old, and weren't even popular then, seen models flash their tits so the bartender would buy them shots. It's a nice place to be, but even three glasses of Dewar's in I'm not having fun.

"Where r u?" Anna texts.

"Bar"

It's packed, but I've been here long enough that I have a seat and I'm not going to stand up and let someone else take it from me. I wave Anna down as she walks in. She stands behind me.

The day has taken its toll on her makeup. Her forehead is sweaty and she's no longer carrying a handful of fliers. It's possible, at the rate she was going, that they're all gone already. She pushes my backpack into my lap, causing me to spill my drink.

"We're leaving."

It's the only thing she can say that can get a rise out of me.

"What! Why?" People are looking at us. Fuck 'em, let them look.

"Come on, we're through," she says, pulling at my arm.

"No, no. I know it's weird but the bar's the best part," I say. I'm drunk, don't want to go anywhere. "You're just tired. Here, take my seat."

I stand and put my hand on her waist, she is sweaty, moist. She doesn't move as I try to guide her down to the bar stool.

She lowers her voice, it's a very specific tone that I've only heard once before.

*Don't you dare cut that camera.*

"You're not understanding me. We need to leave now."

My hands are still wet, I look down at them. They're pink. Her whole tanktop has been soaked and wrung out, I can see the sharp creases where it folded against itself, trying to squeeze out the water. And the blood.

"What did you do," I shout, no longer aware that we're in a crowded bar. I've never hit a woman. I've never hit a man, either, just schoolyard push-fights when I was a kid. I shove her now, both hands flat on her shoulder, one low enough that I touch tit.

It's a push violent enough to send some of the guys out of their seats. I raise both hands above my head, surrendering before anything even starts. I hope no one can see that my hands are tinged pink.

The push causes something to break in Anna's eyes, is some kind of last straw.

"I'll be in the car," she says.


"The retarded guy?" I ask, feeling like I know the answer even though I've got no proof. It could have been anyone, really. I've heard stories of guys trying stuff at conventions, especially with girls in costume, but I also know that Anna is the wrong target.

She doesn't answer me, just drives. She's crying.

I cried plenty, after Burt, but I've never seen a single tear from her, didn't know it was possible until now.

"It wasn't supposed to end like this."

End? The word sobers me, literally and figuratively. We've been getting away with murder so well that I forgot that isn't the norm.

"It's not the end. Don't talk like that. We can go back, clean up whatever you did."

The car accelerates, it's not like when we were driving out here, not Cat Killer at the wheel, but a distraught Anna Friedman.

"Think about it," I say, talking fast, matching the car. "What better place to try and hide something like that, we can walk him right out to the car. No one will bat an eye."

"Now you have ideas?" She says. "Now you think, now you plan? Am I a star yet?"

I don't know what to say, I burp and vomit coats the back of my throat. It tastes like cheap scotch.

We're doomed. She's doomed us.

We're on Sunrise Highway now, back on Long Island but still a long way from home. It's a Friday night, there are enough cars on the road that Anna has to weave, thread through them.

"You're right," I say, my voice pathetic. "What are we going to do?"

The lights on the highway are orange, not replaced to the bright white fluorescents you see elsewhere. The amber gives the pavement a sickly hue. They're passing us fast, too fast.

I check my seatbelt, then hug my backpack to my chest, even though it's not attached to anything, the weight makes me feel safe.

"You're not doing anything. I'm doing everything." She says, jerks the wheel. I know we're off the ground, weightless for a moment, but after that I can't see or feel anything. Or maybe I just can't remember.

## TWENTY-THREE

I keep thinking that I'm going to recognize one of the cops that stream in and out of the room. That I'll see one who was at my house that time that my mother called them. I don't, though. That would be too over the top, even for a movie like this.

My wrist aches, but so does the rest of me.

Speaking of over the top, the handcuffs are a bit much, it's not like I'm going to wake up, broken leg and codeine-filled and stage a daring escape, maybe take out a guard or two.

They tell me that I may even get charged for her, too, sent through the window like a bullet. As drunk as I was when they find us, how agitated I was at the bar, how everyone saw me push her: that's manslaughter, right? They ask me, like I'm the expert.

They know that that first one was her. Well at least they think that Burt was the first one. No denying that one was her, they have the video, of course. But they also think that I forced her to do it somehow, either through direct or indirect coercion. The rest of them? The old man, the retard, her *own* mother. Those they're not so sure, there's fingerprints that link me to one of them, to the Bowie knife, they don't tell me which. I think of the latex, Anna waking me up in the basement, and I can figure out which.

The Kickstarter is cancelled, so I can't use the money to get a lawyer any better than the public defender. The page is down, but I bet video-captured versions of Burt's death are still being handed around on the internet, now that it's infamous, probably by sickos with screennames that I recognize.

My lawyer may as well not be in the room as they talk to me. They don't need me to corroborate any facts, they're just telling me what they think. There are falsehoods, of course, but I'm more shocked by the things that they guess right.

In their story, I've killed them all, in one way or another. They've even been able to dig up my mom's 911 call from all those years ago. There's a computer for those things.

As soon as I'm ready to sit in the box, on trial, they'll peg me for all of it.

And why not?

They're not getting her side of the story and you can't trust mine.

Look at me. The stuff I buy, the shit I've made. I'm the first one you expect.

ABOUT THE AUTHOR:

Adam Cesare is a New Yorker who lives in Philadelphia. He studied English and film at Boston University.

His books include *Video Night*, *The Summer Job* and *Tribesmen*. His nonfiction has appeared in *Paracinema*, *Fangoria*, *The LA Review of Books* and other venues.

# ACKNOWLEDGEMENTS

I wrote this soon after moving to Philadelphia (although it was the second book I completed here), so a shout-out must be given to the people who showed me all the cool places to hang out in the city: Scott Cole and Matt Garrett. And, of course, to Jennifer, for introducing me to my new home.

As usual, big thanks to anyone who has read and liked my stuff well enough to write a review or tell a friend about it. It helps immeasurably. An equally large thank you to the reviewers/bloggers who have supported and discussed my work, most especially Gabino Iglesias and Sean Leonard (who I didn't remember to thank in the last one of these).

Whether you loved this book or you were pissed off that it didn't have any space aliens in it, you can blame its existence entirely on J David Osborne who told me via Facebook message that I: "should write a book...for Broken River. *thunderclaps*"

Printed in Great Britain
by Amazon